HALLOWILLOWEEN
NEFARIOUS SILLINESS FROM CALEF BROWN

Houghton Mifflin Books for Children
Houghton Mifflin Harcourt
Boston New York 2010

For Kane Madigan

All rights reserved. For information about permis-
sion to reproduce selections from this book, write to
Permissions, Houghton Mifflin Harcourt Publishing Com-
pany, 215 Park Avenue South, New York, New York 10003.
Houghton Mifflin Books for Children is an imprint of Houghton
Mifflin Harcourt Publishing Company.
www.hmhbooks.com
The text of this book is set in Arlt.
The illustrations were done in acrylic.
Library of Congress Cataloging-in-Publication Data
Brown, Calef.
Hallowilloween : nefarious silliness from Calef Brown / by Calef Brown.
p. cm.
ISBN 978-0-547-21540-2
1. Children's poetry, American. I. Title.
PS3552.R68525H36 2010
811'.54—dc22
2009049698
Printed in China
LEO 10 9 8 7 6 5 4 3 2 1
4500221873

JACK
LONE STAR WITCHES
HALLOWILLOWEEN
THE OOMPACHUPA LOOMPACABRA
THE VUMPIRE
CAT BATTLE
GRIM SUPPER
DUNCAN
OLD NAPOLEON
THE POLTERGEYSER
NOT FRANKENSTEIN
SCARECROW'S EPITAPH
MUMMY UNHAPPY
THE PORTRAIT OF GORY RENÉ

JACK

Jack is a rare wolf.
A covered with hair wolf.
A crouch in the doorway
to give you a scare wolf.
A big as a bear wolf.
A devil may care wolf.
A constantly burping
and fouling the air wolf.
A give you a glare wolf.
A likely to swear wolf.
A jump up and down
on your favorite chair wolf.
A look over there wolf.
A try not to stare wolf.
A surely by now
you are fully aware wolf
that Jack is a werewolf.

LONE STAR WITCHES

The Witches of Texas
are practicing hexes
in comical conical ten-gallon hats.
They live under bridges
with thousands of bats.
Slobbering bloodhounds
are chasing their cats.

The Witches of Texas,
with cackles and hoots,
are doing a two-step
in lizard-skin boots
while filling a cauldron
with truffles and newts.
A sinister potion
is brewing in Austin
to fire up the feud
with the Witches of Boston.

HALLOWILLOWEEN

Within a hollow willow tree
behind the village green,
busy ants are making plans
for Hallowilloween.
They gather bits of candle wax.
They peel a tangerine.
They decorate the window shades
on Hallowilloween.
A magic night for eager ants:
The spooky games.
The crazy dance.
The rows of cakes and sugared figs.
The costume ball with masks and wigs.
A lucky ant will win a prize
presented by the queen.
The rowdy crowd
will jump and shout
on Hallowilloween.

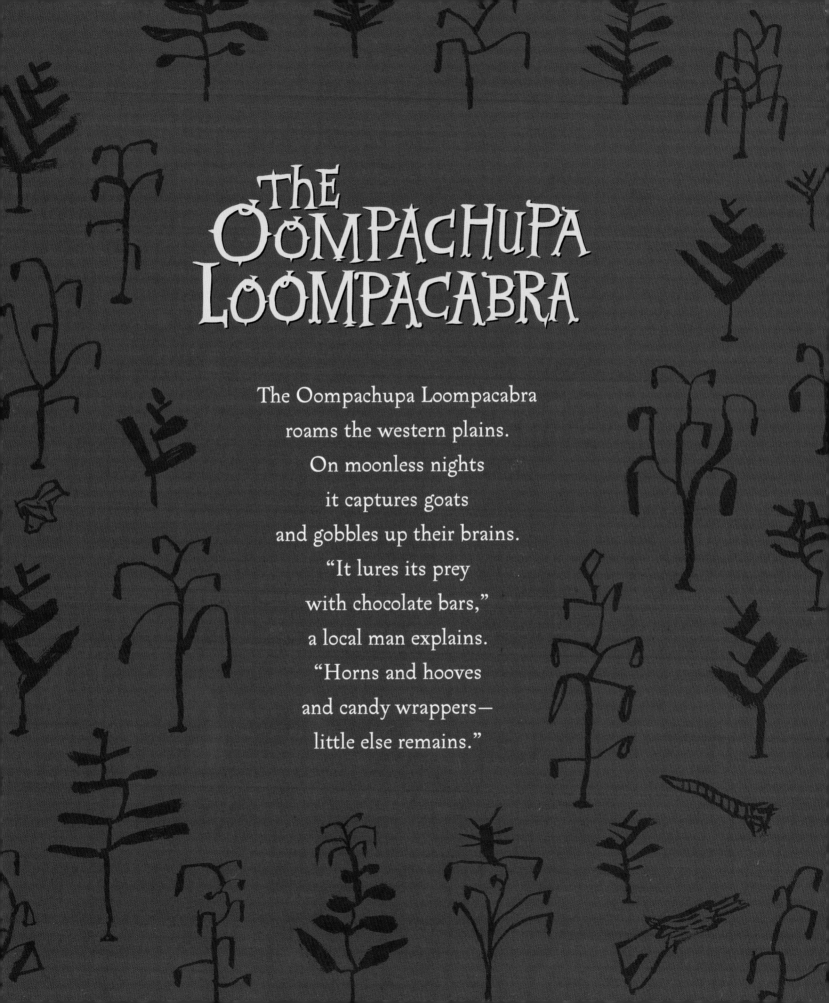

THE OOMPACHUPA LOOMPACABRA

The Oompachupa Loompacabra
roams the western plains.
On moonless nights
it captures goats
and gobbles up their brains.
"It lures its prey
with chocolate bars,"
a local man explains.
"Horns and hooves
and candy wrappers—
little else remains."

THE VUMPIRE

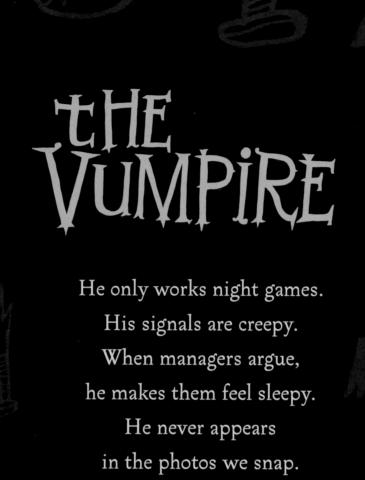

He only works night games.
His signals are creepy.
When managers argue,
he makes them feel sleepy.
He never appears
in the photos we snap.
A widow's peak peeks out
from under his cap
when he takes a nap
in the dugout.
His eyes bug out
and he hisses like a frightened cat
at the sight of a broken bat.
How weird is that?
Once, while waiting on deck,
I caught him staring
at the back of the catcher's neck.

CAT
BATTLE

On All Hallows Eve,
if you happen to see
two alley cats
about to battle,
take heed!
Don't dawdle!
Those fools who meddle
or get in the middle
end up in the hospital,
covered in cat spittle.

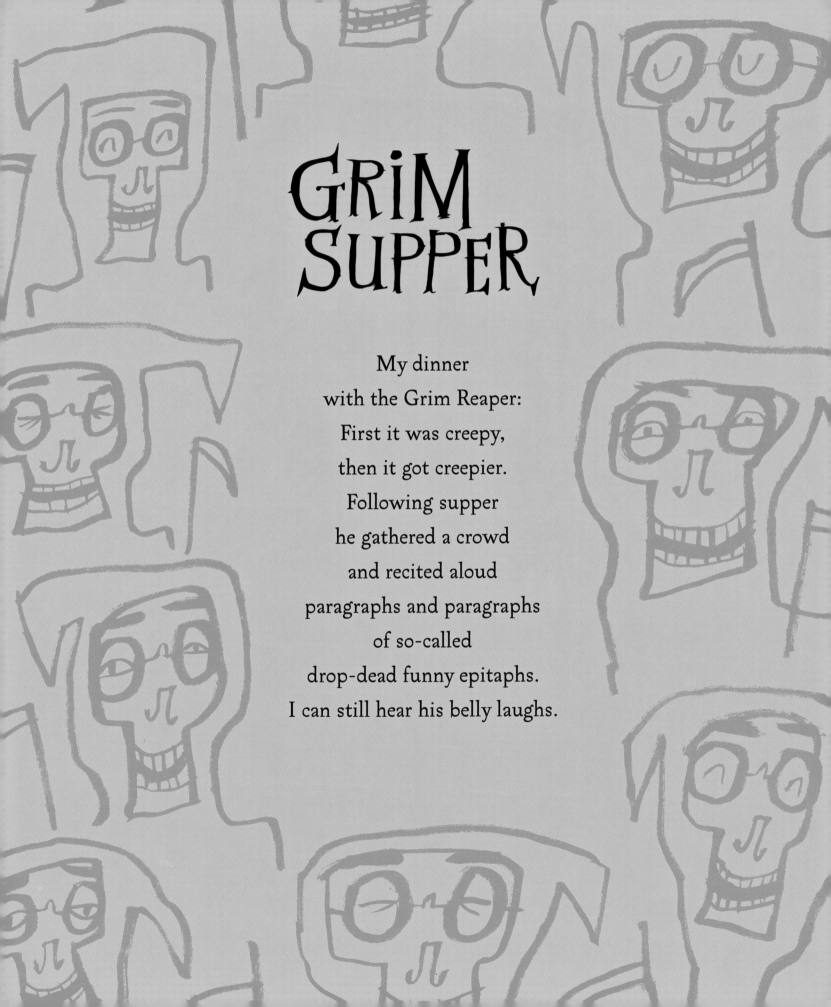

GRiM SUPPER

My dinner
with the Grim Reaper:
First it was creepy,
then it got creepier.
Following supper
he gathered a crowd
and recited aloud
paragraphs and paragraphs
of so-called
drop-dead funny epitaphs.
I can still hear his belly laughs.

DUNCAN

Meet Duncan
the shrunken head.
He has, of course,
no limbs or torso.
He doesn't walk
or ride a horse, so,
a friendly grackle
flies him around.
From high in the sky
they buzz the town,
swooping down
and terrifying passersby.
When children cry,
oh my, how they cackle!
Then the grackle rustles up
some tea, a cup,
and pumpkin bread
to share with Duncan
the shrunken head.

OLD NAPOLEON

An ancient tree
with one dead branch
standing alone
on a tarantula ranch.
This is the home
and humble haven
of Old Napoleon
the hungry raven
who gorges on spiders
each day at lunchtime.
Munch munch munch.
He calls it "crunch time."

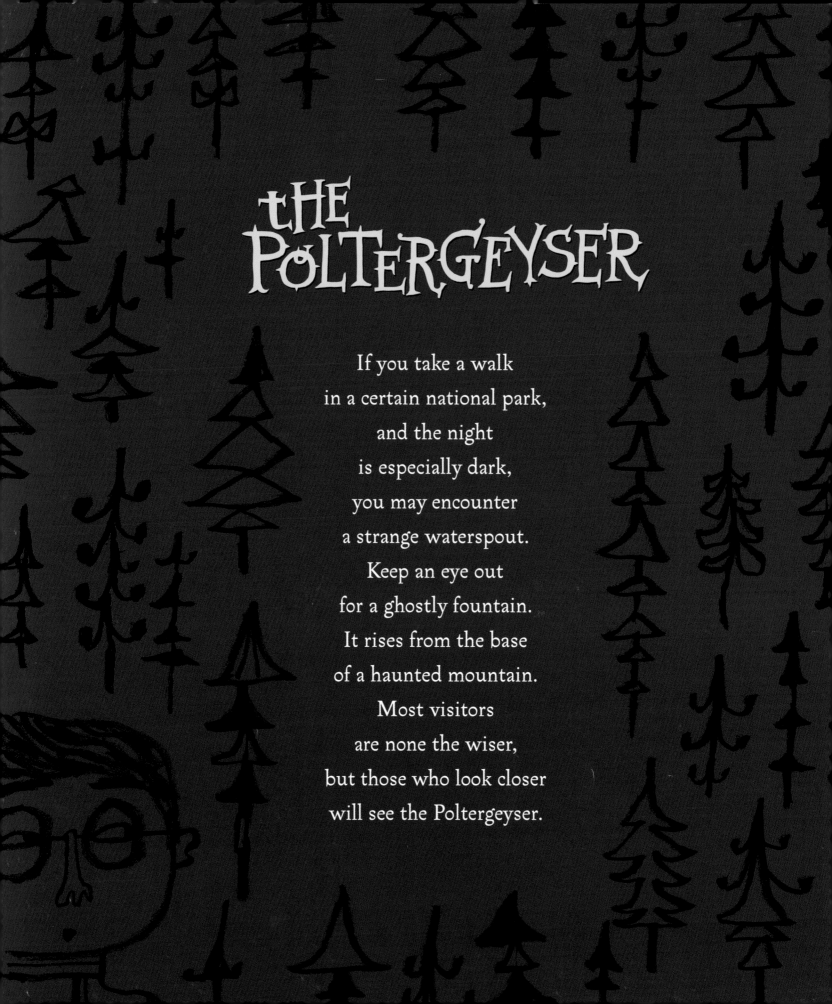

tHE POLTERGEYSER

If you take a walk
in a certain national park,
and the night
is especially dark,
you may encounter
a strange waterspout.
Keep an eye out
for a ghostly fountain.
It rises from the base
of a haunted mountain.
Most visitors
are none the wiser,
but those who look closer
will see the Poltergeyser.

NOT FRANKENSTEIN

I'm not Frankenstein,
but people say
I'm "Frankensteinesque."
I sit at a desk
in my mountain lodge
and do decoupage.
It's an homage, you see,
to the human collage—that's me!
I'm completely assembled
with spare parts.
My head is square
where my hair starts.
My gruff talk,
my stiff walk,
even the way
I sometimes "go ballistic"...
It's all very "Frankensteinistic."

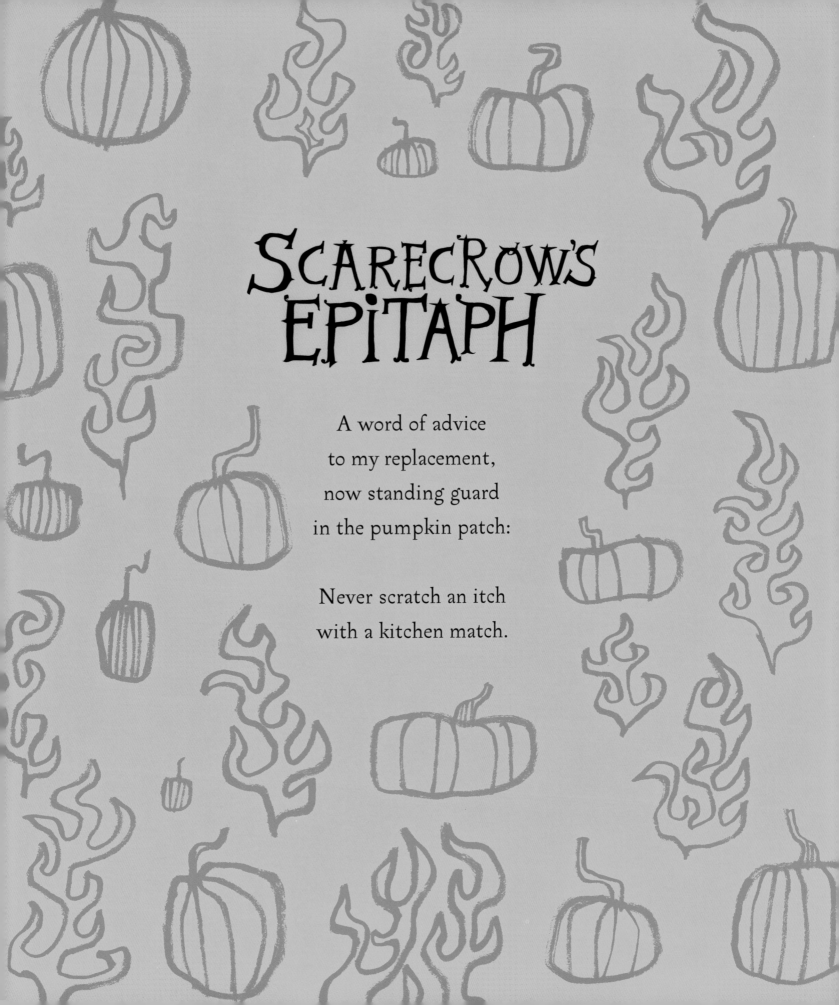

Scarecrow's Epitaph

A word of advice
to my replacement,
now standing guard
in the pumpkin patch:

Never scratch an itch
with a kitchen match.

Mummy Unhappy

"What a bummer!"
the mummy cried.
"Why oh why
was I so badly mummified!
Where is the pride
in good mummification?
I know that it takes
at least *some* education.
Who do I sue?
I'm completely unraveling!
No more vacations.
Forget about traveling.
All of my wrappings
are ragged and ripped.
I slipped up and tripped
on the edge of my crypt!
I totally got gypped,"
the mummy sighed.
"Why oh why
was I so badly mummified?"

THE PORTRAIT OF GORY RENÉ

The horrible portrait
of Gory René—
it perfectly captured
his awful decay.
Portrayed at his worst
in disgusting attire,
for hours and hours
René would admire
his festering sores
and his hideous mange,
so faithfully rendered.
But something was strange—
the face in the painting
was starting to change . . .

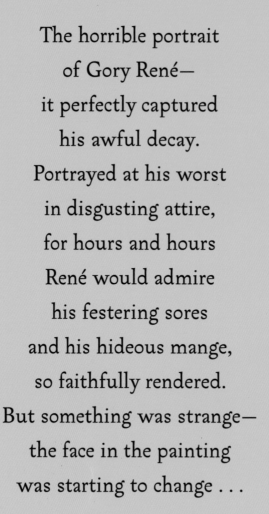

. . . from gruesome to handsome
with each passing day.
Ashamed and embarrassed,
he hid it away.
Concealed in an attic
is where it will stay—
the beautiful portrait
of Gory René.